GAVIN

£4.50
UK only

Written by Bugs Bunny, with a little help from writers John Broadhead and Joyce McAleer

THIS CARROT BELONGS TO

Name ....a.man.d.a......

Address/Hutch 3.2.Foxbur.x

G.rove

cl 4

Hi-ya, Doc . . . glad to have you with us! Now before you start reading, don't forget to fill in this little box, will you? Enjoy the book!

illustrated by Clic! Publishing

design by John Taggart

Published in Great Britain by World International Publishing Limited, an Egmont Company, Egmont House, PO Box 111, Great Ducie Street, Manchester M60 3BL.

Printed in Italy

ISBN 0 7498 0272 3

LOONEY TUNES
ANNUAL 1992

Contents

Bugs Bunny

What can we say about Bugs? He's a handsome, stylish, clever, witty superstar . . . and he has the whitest teeth in Hollywood! Is that everything you told me to say, Bugs? Whoops, sorry!
Likes: Carrots, carrots and more carrots.
Hates: Running out of carrots!

Sylvester

Gee, what a great guy! Sylvester tells us he can't stand to see a creature kept behind bars. That must be why he's taking Tweety out of his cage right now. Hey, stop it, cat — and scat!
Likes: Helping little old ladies and feeding birds.
Hates: Dogs with sharp teeth and birds with loud squawks.

Tweety

Cute and cuddly with the sweetest voice you've ever heard! You can't help but love Tweety . . . there's nothing nasty about him! Even after all those narrow escapes, he still thinks Sylvester is his best friend!
Likes: Singing Love is the Tweetest Thing.
Hates: Nothing!

Porky Pig

Good old Porky! He often gets into trouble on his adventures with Bugs, but he always bounces back. No wonder — he's built like a rubber ball!
Likes: Having a cool shower — a pig-swill!
Hates: Playing piggy in the middle, because he's always 'it'!

Elmer Fudd

There goes Elmer! He may be a good buddy of Bugs some of the time . . . but if there's one thing he can't resist, it's a good wabbit-hunt! Think he has a big head? Nope, he's just got a tiny body!
Likes: Watching Nightmare on Elmer Street.
Hates: Words with a letter 'r' in them!

Daffy Duck

Why is he called Daffy? You'll soon know when you get to meet him! He's a genius at thinking up clever ideas — trouble is, none of them ever works. He's just as daffy as a brush!
Likes: The Adventures of Sir Francis Drake.
Hates: Ducking-stools and Mrs Beeton's Duckery Book!

Yosemite Sam

Aharr, look out, shipmates . . . it be Yosemite Sam, the roughest, toughest pirate that ever sailed the seven . . . er . . . boating lakes! Careful you don't trip over your moustache, Sam!
Likes: Walking the dog.
Hates: Walking the plank!

Road Runner

Sorry there's no picture of Road Runner: he was too fast even to photograph!
Likes: Breaking the sound-barrier!
Hates: Police speed-traps!

Wile E. Coyote

Hey, Coyote's no oil-painting — it really is him! Try putting your brakes on sooner, pal, and watch out for walls!
Likes: Long-distance running.
Hates: Long-distance falling!

Foghorn Leghorn

Ah say, ah say, ah say — hold on, is that all Foghorn can say? His voice is loud enough to wake everyone for miles at dawn — well, it would be, if he'd learn to tell the time and not oversleep!
Likes: The sound of his own voice!
Hates: Being called 'chicken'!

Pepe Le Pew

Wow, what a niff! Perhaps he should really be called Pepe Le *Phewww*! We all know skunks make a smell to keep their enemies away, but it's a wonder Pepe has any friends left!
Likes: Ping-pong!
Hates: Deodorant!

Tasmanian Devil

We don't know much about the Tasmanian Devil, except that he's . . . er . . . from Tasmania . . . probably. You see, no one's ever dared to get close enough to him to
Likes: Eating.
Hates: Everything else!

Porky Pig sat at an old desk in the cold, miserable classroom and shivered.

"Oh, d-dear," he mumbled. "I wish I hadn't agreed to be the first p-pupil at Daffy's new school. I hate being up so early!"

But it was too late, because at that moment Daffy Duck strode into the room and took his place at the teacher's desk. He was all in black — black gown, black cap and black feathers!

"H-hi there, Daffy!" smiled Porky, trying to sound cheerful.

"Whaddyamean by that?!" snarled Daffy, striding over to Porky and towering over him, beak to snout. "Call me 'Sir' in future. Okay?"

"O-okay, S-sir!"

Daffy returned to his desk and opened a big red book. "I'd better start the register," he announced. "What's your name, boy?"

"M-my name?" asked Porky, looking round in surprise. "Why, you know my name, Daffy . . . I mean *Sir*!"

Daffy slapped down his pen in temper and made a big blot on his nice clean page. "*Name*, boy!"

"P-porky, Sir!"

"Porky what? Porky Pine?"

"P-porky Pig, Sir!"

"That's more like it, kid!" Daffy began to write, then stopped. "Hmmm, how many 'g's in Pig?"

And so the morning went on — very slowly for poor old Porky, as he discovered that he was the *only* pupil in Daffy's school. He was class monitor, of course, and had to do all the fetching and carrying for his bad-tempered teacher. At least he had lunchtime to look forward to . . . until he found out that Daffy had forgotten to organize any school meals!

So he sat in silence with a glass of water and dreamed of lots to eat. And then he had a bright idea! He jumped up quickly and raced to a telephone box in the hallway. There he dialled the number of a certain friend . . .

Wow, were things *different* after lunch! When Porky returned to his lessons, Daffy had changed completely. He actually smiled as he helped Porky to his desk. Then he gave him a cushion to sit on and sharpened all his pencils for him!

"Must make a good impression," he muttered, cleaning the blackboard with the end of his gown. "Got an important visitor coming!"

Halfway through the geography lesson, Porky pointed out a mistake. "N-no, Sir, New Orleans isn't the capital of France — it's *Paris*!"

"Okay, if you say so . . . Paris it is!" beamed Daffy. He passed Porky a piece of chocolate and patted him on the head.

Porky spent the next couple of hours in luxury! He lay back on a sun-chair, with a box of chocolates and a cool glass of lemonade by his side.

Suddenly a knock came at the door and in strode a rich-looking fellow in a white suit and brimmed hat. Under his wide drooping moustache he had a familiar toothy grin.

Daffy sprang up and ran to the man, shaking his hand vigorously. "Why, you must be Mr Mortimer Moneybags! Pleased to meet you," he smiled. "Now, please take a look round my luxury school. Your son, Mortimer Junior, will love it here. *All* the pupils do!"

"*Pupils?*" asked Mr Moneybags, peering all around through a monocle held to his eye. "Why, ah kin see only *one!*"

"Well, small classes mean a better education for your boy," gushed Daffy.

Mr Moneybags held out his monocle and looked Daffy up and down. And, as he did so, Daffy thought he'd seen that silly grin before. He stroked his beak thoughtfully.

"What's up, Doc?" asked Mr Moneybags.

"Oh, nothing, I just thought your face seemed — *hey*, what was that you said?"

"What? *What's up, Doc?*" repeated Mr Moneybags.

Daffy's beak turned red with rage. He grabbed Mr Moneybags' moustache and pulled it off! He snatched the hat off his head and gasped as two long rabbit's ears popped up!

"*Bugs Bunny!* So this was all a plot to make life easy for Porky Pig, huh?!" he cried, picking up a swishy cane. "Lesson one's about to start: don't fool with the teacher."

Bugs and Porky didn't wait for the end-of-school bell! Within five seconds they were out of the building and fleeing across the playing field with Daffy Duck in hot pursuit.

I don't expect that Porky will be back at his desk tomorrow, do you?

ROAD RUNNER

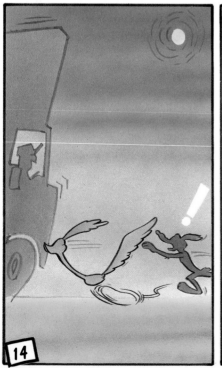

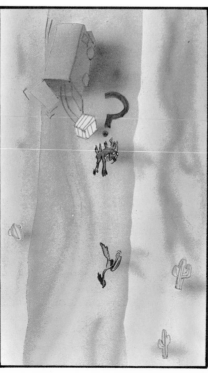

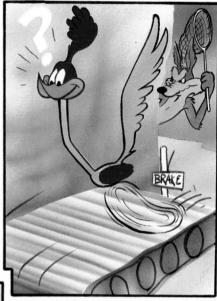

15

Bugs' World

Hi-ya, folks, it's Bugs here! Now, if you like readin' tales about the past — or even if you don't! — you'll love my mini history lesson!

No kidding, my ancestors and their carrots have played a big part in the story of our planet. Back in the mists of time, for example, when rabbits had only just been invented, ol' Ugh Bug lived in . . . a cave, of all things! They called him Ugh Bug 'cos "Ugh Bug" was all he ever said. But he was no goof. Who d'ya think grew the very first carrot?!

Then, movin' on a few hundred thousand years, there was good ol' Bugustus Caesar, Emperor of Rome — an' anywhere else he could lay his paw on! He never did much; he just lazed around all day, being fed carrots by his servants. They say that he just carried on eating carrots as Rome burned!

Hey, remember those great adventures about the outlaw Robin Hood? Well, they got the name wrong . . . it was really Rabbit Hood! He an' his

History

pals lived in a hideout at the heart of Sherwood Forest, right enough, but all they ever stole from the rich was . . . carrots! They tried giving them to the poor, but they were sick of carrots. So Rabbit Hood an' his buddies just ate them themselves! You'll read more about them later in this annual.

Now to more recent history! You've probably heard of Napoleon Bunnyparte, the French conqueror who was famous for keeping a hand inside his jacket. What d'ya think he was doin'? Holdin' an ice-lolly? Keepin' his hand warm? No danger, Doc . . . he was simply keepin' a spare carrot ready in case he got peckish on the battlefield!

Finally to bring us right up to date, who d'ya think was the first person to walk on the Moon? Neil Armstrong? He was the first *man*, yep, but he never mentioned the rabbit footprints he found there, did he? An' who d'you think left 'em there? Yours truly, of course!

See you around!

Bugs' Best Jokes

How do you attract rabbits to your garden?

– Make a noise like a carrot!

What do you get if you cross a rabbit with a sheep?

– A woolly jumper!

What's another name for a rabbit's umbrella?

– A hare-dryer!

What will go up down, but not down up?

– An umbrella in a chimney!

What's another name for a London Underground train full of professors?

– A tube of Smarties!

Why did the zoo-keeper call at the garage?

– The Jaguar needed an MOT!

Where do rich bunnies live?

– In the burrow of Mayfair!

Why do storks stand on one leg?

– If they didn't they'd fall over

What do you call someone with a rabbit sticking out of each ear?

– Warren?

Why do foxes look so well-groomed?

– They always have a brush with them!

How do we know that eating carrots is good for the eyesight?

– Ever seen a rabbit wearing glasses!?

18

DEVIL in the SKY!

Did you ever hear of Bugs Bunny's adventures as an airline pilot? No? That's probably because he didn't last very long at the job! Let's find out why he got the sack . . .

Bugs was working for Bobtail Airways at the time. He'd just arrived in London when the boss asked him to fly a special guest to Tasmania. *Tasmania*, thought Bugs, sounds familiar – but where had he heard of it before?

He should have guessed there was something strange when he was told that the passenger would be travelling inside a huge wooden crate in the goods compartment!

Anyway, Captain Bugs was zooming through the clouds towards Tasmania when he remembered that his special guest hadn't eaten. So he sent his trusty steward Porky Pig with a snack tray. That was his big mistake!

Five minutes later the pilot's cabin door burst open with a bang, almost making Bugs jump out of his rabbit-skin!

"Shh, Doc, you're keeping me awake!" he joked, thinking it was Porky returning.

Chomp! A huge shapeless lump with gnashing teeth lurched forward and ate the entire co-pilot's seat in one gulp.

"Hey, that was someone's seat!" cried Bugs, trying to keep calm as he found himself face to face with the dreaded Tasmanian Devil! "So that's all the thanks I get for buying you lunch!"

Chomp! The Tasmanian Devil's response was to gobble up the steering-wheel. Then he stood back, grinning.

"This could be serious! I jus' hope you don't try anythin' with the engines!" exclaimed Bugs. Then he wished he hadn't spoken!

Chomp! The Devil ate a big hole in the side of the aircraft and bounded out on to the wings. *Chomp*, one tasty engine! The aeroplane slowed down a little. *Chomp*, two tasty engines! The aeroplane went slower still. *Chomp*, three tasty engines! Crumbs, thought Bugs, if he eats the last one, we'll be up here all day!

The aircraft went into a steep dive towards the ground. Having no controls left didn't help, but Bugs remembered that a captain always keeps his cool. He clutched the microphone and began to address his panicking passengers: "This is your Coward – I mean Captain – speaking," he began, but he was interrupted by the

21

Tasmanian Devil, who grabbed the microphone and chewed it up!

Then, licking his lips, the Devil advanced upon Bugs.

"What's up, Doc? You going to eat *me* next?" asked Bugs bravely.

The Devil grunted as if he meant yes, but he didn't get the chance, for at that moment Porky charged into the cabin in a temper!

"And what, may I ask, is going on here?" he demanded angrily. He flicked a switch marked 'Automatic Pilot'. "That should do the trick!"

Immediately the aircraft swung round sharply and began to fly straight. The Devil was knocked off balance and tumbled through the big hole in the side of the cabin!

Down, down he fell and landed with an enormous splash in the sea below.

"That's the l-last we'll s-see of him!" said Porky.

"I doubt it," replied Bugs, watching the Tasmanian Devil swimming for a nearby island.

Bugs took off his cap and placed it firmly on Porky's head, then picked him up and sat him in the pilot's seat. "*You're* the pilot now, Doc. Take us home, will you? *I'm* going for a spot of lunch!"

Here's a lovely picture for you to colour in with crayons, felt-tips or coloured pencils! It's me having breakfast with my best friend, Sylvester the puddy-tat! Strange, but I had a funny feeling that he wanted the key to my cage . . . I wonder why?!

FOGHORN LEGHORN in
FARMYARD OF THE FUTURE

Y'know, Foghorn... this place is such a dreary dump, it's a wonder the chickens don't all go on **STRIKE**!

You're not kidding, Henery! Ah say, you're not kidding!

Well, lookee here, ah say! Our ol' pal Bugs Bunny has jus' made a fortune on the Stock Exchange – and he's sent us a present!

£1,000

Good ol' Bugs!

Bugs WHO?

This could be our lucky break!

THIS MONEY FROM BUGS COMES IN HANDY...

You won't know the place when the work's finished! Ah say, you won't know...

It's okay, Fogs, we all heard you the **FIRST** time!

Tee hee!

Finished at last – and it's all yours! There ain't **NEVER** been a farmyard like it!

You can say **THAT** again!

Don't encourage him! Hee!

FOGHORN'S FARMYARD OF THE FUTURE IS FINE AT FIRST...

BUT SOON...

My video's on the blink, Foghorn!

I'll ring the repair shop...

25

Puzzle parade

Elmer's word box

```
T W E E L G O T T D E S
C T S Y L D A F F Y L E
R W F O G H U O O O M L
P E P E R A B U G S E I
G E P O R G E R H S R X
F T E L M O T P O R K Y
S Y L V E S T E R S I D
T W I D D L U F N B U D
```

Can you find me and the other names below in my word box? Look carefully – across and downwards!

ELMER   PEPE
BUGS   PORKY
DAFFY   SYLVESTER
FOGHORN   TWEETY

Sylvester's spot-the-difference

Sylvester's photos may look the same, but there are six little differences. Try to spot them!

Porky's bricks

Whoops! Bugs has crashed into Porky's house and left a large hole in the wall! How many bricks will Porky need to fill the gap?

All at sea with Sam!

Here's a great trick to fool your friends! Say to 'em:

"There are thirty sick sailors on a ship. Ten go ashore to see the doctor. How many are left?"

Nearly everyone will get it wrong and guess twenty-six — because they'll think you're saying thirty-six sailors instead of thirty sick sailors!

Take Tweety home

Help Tweety back to the cage — without meeting Sylvester on the way!

The boys have gone kite-flying but the strong wind has tangled up their strings. Can you work out who is flying which kite?

Turn to page 61 for the answers.

Kite plight!

A

C

B

D

1   2   3   4

27

Pepe Le Pew in
PEPE'S MISGUIDED TOUR

"Bonjour, everyone! Welcome to Paris! And welcome to Pepe's Guided Tours!" announced Pepe Le Pew, standing at the foot of the huge Eiffel Tower.

He was talking to his party of tourists, which consisted of Bugs, Porky, Daffy and Elmer! Bugs had decided to treat his pals to a little continental holiday.

"Here we 'ave zee magnificent Eiffel Tower," continued Pepe. "Eet was built one 'undred years ago and stands more than . . . er . . . well, eet is pretty high, as you see."

Porky looked up. "Why is it c-called the Eiffel Tower?"

"Oh . . . um . . . because eet is such an eyeful, of course!" explained Pepe, who didn't know that it was named after Monsieur Eiffel. "Let us move on now, eef you please!"

As the group walked away, Porky was still gazing in wonder at the enormous tower. And when he glanced round, everyone had disappeared! "Oh, n-no! Where'd they go?" he cried.

Pepe and the others arrived at the River Seine. He pointed out the famous left bank of the river, where artists were busily painting pictures.

"Bank?" said Elmer, screwing up his eyes to see. "That's handy. I'll draw out some cash with my cwedit card." And he wandered off to find the bank!

Next, Pepe took his party to the Louvre Museum, home of

the famous Mona Lisa picture.

"See 'ow she smiles at me," said Pepe shyly. "She is adorable, n'est-ce pas? She was painted by Leonardo da Vinci, who also made helicopters . . . and . . . um . . . sports cars, I think!"

Bugs admired the classic painting, but Daffy wasn't impressed. He preferred another painting, entitled *Ducks in Flight over Hollywood.* "Hmm, bet there's some rich pickings there, all right!" he murmured to himself, not noticing Pepe and Bugs leaving the gallery!

Finally, Pepe wove his way expertly through the busy Paris streets. "Now I shall take you all to my favourite bistro for some delicious . . ."

Bugs was alarmed by

Pepe's sudden expression of alarm. "What's up, Doc?" he enquired.

"There is only you and me left! Where are zee others?"

"Hey, you're right, pal!" laughed Bugs. "Looks like they've split. Hope they paid you for the tour!"

"Oui, oui!" nodded Pepe. "But I cannot leave zem lost in zee city. What shall I do?"

Bugs twitched his nose and scratched his ears, then at last gave a toothy grin. "I've got it — but you won't like it!"

"I don't care! Just go ahead!"

"Okay, if you insist!" agreed Bugs. He pushed his nose against Pepe's, stared into his eyes and yelled in his loudest, blood-curdling voice, "BOOOOOO!"

Pepe leapt back in shock. Then something began to happen! Know what happens when skunks get scared? They give off a dreadful scent to scare away their enemies — and that's just what Pepe did!

People on the pavement scattered, holding their noses; car drivers honked their horns, wound up their windows and raced off to avoid the pong!

"Why did you do zat?" demanded Pepe angrily.

"I knew you wouldn't like it, but I think it'll work!" giggled Bugs.

And it did! Porky by the Eiffel Tower, Elmer by the Seine, and Daffy still in the Louvre sniffed at the ghastly odour. Realizing that it was caused by Pepe, they followed their noses — and after five minutes found their way back to their skunk-guide and Bugs.

"Sorry, I cannot take you for a meal," said Pepe sadly, gesturing towards the bistro nearby.

Bugs, Porky, Daffy, Elmer looked and saw the chef, with a peg on his nose, pinning up a sign which said: "Closed — for good!"

"Never mind," said Bugs. "We'll pick up some carrots!"

"Ugh!" cried everyone else!

Who Burgled Bugs?

A solve-it-yourself MYSTERY

See if you can discover whodunnit in this little play acted out by some very familiar faces!

Inspector Fuddprint has been called in to investigate a burglary at Bugs' country house. He has rounded up the local rascals for questioning . . .

"This afternoon at two o'clock there was a wobbery here — and one of you must have done it!" snaps Inspector Fuddprint.

"Oh, dear!" purrs Sinister Sylvester with a sneer. "But it wasn't me. I've been watching TV all day with Tweety Sly."

"It's true!" chirps Tweety Sly.

"I see," hisses Fuddprint. "And what about you, Dirty Duck?"

"I'm completely innocent," says Dirty Duck. "Anyway, I've got pots of money. What would I want with a measly £20?"

"It w-wasn't me either," whines Perilous Porky nervously. "I was at the chemist's getting medicine for my auntie! You can check if you like!"

"Don't blame me. Ah say, don't blame me!" flaps Fingers Foghorn. "I was . . . er . . . strolling in the park by myself at two o'clock! You'll have to look elsewhere for your thief!"

"You're wrong, my dear Fingers!" cackles Fuddprint. "The culprit is in this woom — and I know exactly who he is!"

Well, who is it? The answer is on page 61.

BUT THAT NIGHT...

Bah! If ye poke me with your elbows again, I'll clap ye in irons!

SHHH, Cap'n!

Y-You were right, Bugs! They've come back!

Okay, Porky! I've got my disguise ready. Switch on the searchlight...

WOO...WOOOOOOO!

AAARGH! Let's ged outta here!

Shiver me timbers!

Well, what have we here?

It's TREASURE, B-Bugs...straight ahead!

HEY, what gives?

WHAT a c-catch!

Jumpin' jack-wabbits - a WEAL tweasure-chest! I've found some wicked piwate's fortune!

W-Where did it go?

I'm too cold to care, Porky!

BOY, OH BOY...Now I can buy a gweat big boat!

33

Sylvester and Tweety in

CAGEY CAT!

Sylvester sat on the window-ledge and watched as Granny waved to him and rode away in the taxi. He waited until she had disappeared from sight, then jumped down and rubbed his paws in glee.

"Hee, hee! Now it's time to watch the birdie!" he chuckled. "Alone at last with Tweety — and for a whole morning!"

Tweety, sitting in his cage on the kitchen table, was enjoying the warm sunshine that poured through the bars. He was whistling a sweet tune but he stopped when Sylvester's nose and beady eyes appeared over the edge of the table.

"Hey," he cheeped. "I tawt I taw a puddy-tat!"

"You did, you did, little guy!" purred Sylvester, reaching for the cage door and licking his lips. "Come on out for a while!"

But the cage door wouldn't open. Sylvester rattled it and then discovered it was fastened with a strong padlock.

"I'm to stay in here while Granny's away," announced Tweety innocently. "She locked me in to keep me safe. But she didn't need to worry — because you're here to look after me!"

"Bah!" hissed Sylvester, disappearing for a moment, then returning with a small saw.

"Why are you trying to cut through my bars?" enquired Tweety.

"Aw, shut your beak!" replied Sylvester, panting as he sawed away.

Ding-dong! The doorbell rang and in walked Elmer Fudd.

"Hi there, Sylvester," he cried. "Gwanny asked me to call wound to give you and Tweety your bweakfast."

Sylvester dropped the saw in shock. Elmer bent down and picked it up. "Just what I need," he said, "to wepair my wecord-player."

Sylvester kept a greedy eye on Tweety while Elmer spooned some cat food into his dish and filled up Tweety's bowl with seed.

"Not hungwy, puss?" asked Elmer.

I have something tastier in mind, thought Sylvester, dreaming of a Tweety pie!

At last Elmer left. Sylvester put his tongue out at him behind his back, then returned to Tweety's cage and began to prise open the bars with a large screwdriver.

"What are you doing?" chirped Tweety.

"You need a little more air on a hot day like this!" purred Sylvester.

"Thank you! You're so kind!"

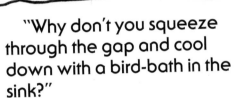

"Why don't you squeeze through the gap and cool down with a bird-bath in the sink?"

"Oh, no, I can't come out. I promised."

Ding-dong! The doorbell rang again, just as Sylvester was reaching into Tweety's cage. The front door burst open and in marched Foghorn Leghorn!

"Good mornin'! Ah say, good mornin', cat!" he boomed. "Jus' lookin' in. Ah say, I'm jus' lookin' in on you and Tweety here while Granny's away."

Foghorn spied Sylvester's screwdriver and then noticed the bent bars of the cage. "Oh, you're tryin' to straighten out Tweety's cage, huh?"

Of course, Sylvester couldn't say no, and he watched angrily as Foghorn pulled the bars together again with his claw.

"I'll borrow this screwdriver. Ah say, I'll borrow this screwdriver, if you don't mind, to fix the hen-house door." And Foghorn swept out of the house.

"If one more person calls round and interrupts me, I'll . . . I'll . . ." shouted Sylvester, fuming with rage! Then he picked up a wooden spoon and rattled it against the cage.

"Is this a new game?" squeaked Tweety gently. "It's a bit noisy!"

Ding-dong! The doorbell sounded yet again.

"That does it!" yelled Sylvester. He picked up a huge pawful of slushy cat food from his dish and flung it at the front door just as it opened.

Splat! It splashed all over Granny, who had arrived back home!

"Oops! Whoops!" yelled Sylvester. Then his cries grew louder and more desperate as Granny chased him from the house with her favourite sweeping-brush. "Ouch! Ye-owww! Aarghh!"

"Poor Sylvester . . . I wonder why he threw his breakfast at Granny?" cheeped Tweety, swinging on his perch. "He's such a thoughtful puddy-tat . . . and so kind to me!"

SAY CARROTS!

What is Bugs up to? You'll find out on page 61.

37

ROAD RUNNER'S RACE

Play this game with friends. You need a counter for each player, and a die. Take turns to shake the die, and move along the track. If you shake a three, move on three squares, and so on. The first player to reach the picnic is the winner. Remember to obey the instructions on some of the squares.

Whoops- you twist your ankle! Say Bugs' favourite phrase five times and miss a turn.

67

66

65

35

36

34

37

Lost in the caves. Shout for help like Porky and miss a turn.

33

Lucky you! The rope bridge takes you on to 66.

38

39

Landslide! Slip back to 35.

32

42

40

41

31

Take a short cut on the mountain railway.

30

29

28

27

26

25

24

23

Rattlesnake! Wait till it goes away. Miss a turn.

Hit your toe on a rock. Make a 'beep, beep' noise like Roadrunner and miss a turn.

1

2

3

4

5

6

69
70
71
73
72
74

Hurry on to 74.

Yippee!

You find scary footprints! Go back to 65.

63
62
61
60
59
58
57
56

Chased by a vulture! Go on to 63.

55

Stop to investigate a secret passage. It takes you back to 44!

Hillbillies! Hide behind a rock and miss two turns.

54

44
45
46
47
48
49
50
51
52
53

Stop to rest. Say your name and address in Elmer's voice and miss a turn.

Coyote is behind you! Run forward to 28.

18
17
16

19
15

21
20
14

A falling rock scares you. Jump forward to 13.

Flooded path slows you down. Sing a nursery rhyme in Tweety's voice and miss a turn.

13

8
9
10
11
12

Bugs Bunny in Up the Creek

The blinding sun shone down on the three horsemen — Bugs, Porky and Elmer Fudd — as they rode into Carrot Creek.

"Here at last!" exclaimed Bugs, climbing from his horse and tying it up outside the Lucky Nugget Saloon.

"W-why is everyone scared of us?" asked Porky, noticing that all the townsfolk had run away.

"Dunno — but I aim to find out," replied Bugs, spotting a young cowboy hiding behind a rain-barrel. He shouted, "What's up, Doc?"

The cowboy walked up slowly with fear in his eyes. "D-don't shoot . . . please!"

"Why should I?" asked Bugs.

"Well, y-you *are* Desperado Dave, ain't ya?"

"Who?!" laughed Bugs. "Listen, pal, I'm Bugs Bunny, your new marshal, an' these are my deputies, Porky Pig and Elmer Fudd."

Porky nodded and Elmer said, "Mornin', pardner."

The cowboy was relieved. "Phew! You're just in time to defend us! Desperado Dave's comin' to shoot up the town at noon!"

Bugs turned to Porky and Elmer. "No wonder we got this job without even an interview!" he sighed, pushing back his hat.

Twelve noon came and Carrot Creek was like a ghost town: everyone was indoors, peeping from behind curtains. And then . . . Desperado Dave arrived!

He was huge and hairy and horrible! Even his horse looked scared of him. He tied it up at the saloon and swaggered over to the marshal's office.

"Ready to defend your town, Marshal?" he bellowed.

From behind the door came Bugs' voice: "Be with you in a mo', pal. I'm jus' washin' some lettuce!"

Desperado Dave hissed with annoyance. "I'll count to three an' then I'll start shootin'!" he cried. "One . . . two . . ."

The door swung open and there stood Bugs looking mean and nasty in a long overcoat that reached to the ground.

"Draw, tough guy!" drawled Dave.

"Draw? Me? I can't – I don't have a pencil!" joked Bugs.

"I said draw!" snarled Dave. "One . . . two . . . three!"

Bang, bang! Bang, bang! Bang, bang! Guns blazed, but they weren't Dave's! Bugs' paws were just a fast blur as he shot the gun from Dave's hand and the hat from his head – and sent it bouncing off down the dusty street!

41

"Ye – oww!" screamed Dave. "I ain't no match fer you! I'm off!"

And off he was, without bothering to take his horse! He raced across the prairie leaving a trail of dust behind him.

"Well done! Bravo! Hurray!" shouted the people from the town, coming to shake Bugs by the hand.

"Aw, thanks a bunch," smiled Bugs coyly, "but it wasn't just me . . ."

"It was m-me too!" announced Porky, appearing smartly from beneath Bugs' long coat and twirling a pair of smoking six-guns.

"Me too!" added a gun-toting Elmer, also stepping out of Bugs' open coat. "Boy, Despewado Dave was wunning scared!"

"The whole town is grateful to you boys – *all* of you!" said the mayor. "Come across to the saloon and have a drink!"

"You got carrot-juice?" asked Bugs.

"All the carrot-juice you'll ever want!" laughed the mayor.

And, cheering loudly, the grateful inhabitants of Carrot Creek carried Bugs, Porky and Elmer high on their shoulders to celebrate in the Lucky Nugget!

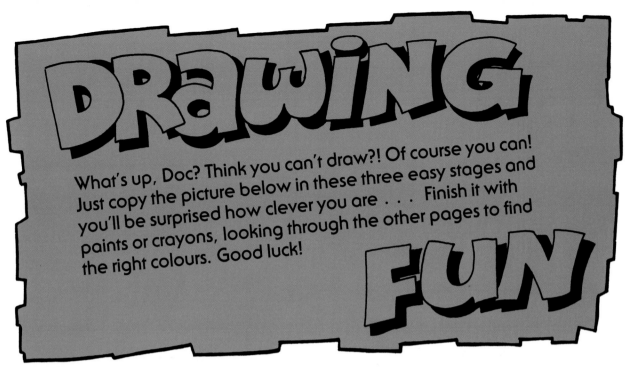

DRAWING FUN

What's up, Doc? Think you can't draw?! Of course you can! Just copy the picture below in these three easy stages and you'll be surprised how clever you are . . . Finish it with paints or crayons, looking through the other pages to find the right colours. Good luck!

BUGS BUNNY in Rabbit Hood

At their secret hideaway, deep in Sherwood Forest, Rabbit Hood and his not-so-Merry Men gathered round the campfire to share a huge carrot pie.

"It's okay for *you*, boss — you like c-carrots!" complained Friar Tuck. "I'd prefer ch-ch-chocolate myself."

"No chance, pal!" scoffed Rabbit Hood with a toothy grin. "Chocolate ain't been invented yet!"

Their laughter was interrupted by Alan-a-Dale rushing breathlessly into camp. "Rabbit . . . Tuck . . . bad news! The Sheriff of Nuttingham has thrown Little John into the castle dungeon!"

"Shucks!" exclaimed Rabbit, continuing to munch his pie. "We'll have to see the Sheriff about this!"

"Now's your chance, Rabbit," panted Alan. "He's coming through the forest at this moment!"

Rabbit sprang to his feet and grabbed his trusty bow and arrow. "We got work to do. Forget the pie, Tuck!"

"With p-pleasure!" cried the tubby Friar.

"What a bumpy wide!" moaned the evil Sheriff, sitting on a cart being pulled by a bony horse.

"Sorry, my lord," mumbled Daffy, his duck-at-arms. Suddenly he pulled hard on the reins and stopped with a jerk. "Drat! It's outlaws!"

In front of them stood Rabbit Hood, carrying a small sack, alongside Friar Tuck and Alan-a-Dale with their bows at the ready.

"What do you want, you pesky wobber?" demanded the Sheriff.

Rabbit looked at the back of the cart. "How about these fresh carrots for the castle kitchen?"

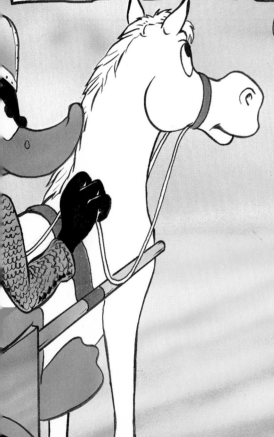

"Cawwots? Is that all?" sighed the Sheriff. "For a minute I thought you knew about the gold coins hidden in my twouser pockets!"

"I know we t-take from the rich and give t-to the poor," said Tuck, "but the village peasants are sick of c-carrots."

But Rabbit had a master plan! Behind the Sheriff's back, he and Friar Tuck dived into the carrots and hid themselves. Then Alan-a-Dale waved the Sheriff on, saying, "Okay, you can go now!"

"About time too," snapped Daffy indignantly.

The Sheriff and Daffy drove into the courtyard of Nuttingham Castle.

"Safe at last!" squawked Daffy, closing the huge gates behind them. But neither of them noticed Tuck and Rabbit scramble from the cart and run down some nearby stone steps!

Down in the dark depths of the dungeons, Rabbit poked his nose through the small, barred window of a heavy door. He saw Little John sitting sadly in the corner of his cell. Little John was a silly name: he was big and strong — and so was his *voice*!

"Rabbit Hood, am ah glad to see you! Ah say, am ah glad to see you!" he boomed.

"Shhh!" whispered Tuck, tugging at the bars. "Oh dear, this d-door's awful strong."

"Move aside," commanded Rabbit. "I have a secret weapon — all the way from France!"

He unfastened the sack he was carrying and out popped *Pepe Le Pew*!

"Alors, what a way to travel!" complained Pepe, brushing his ruffled coat smooth again. "Now, this is le door, n'est-ce pas?"

46

Rabbit nodded, and Pepe climbed up the door and disappeared between the bars.

"What's this? Ah say, what's this?!" cried Little John, as Pepe began to make his terrible nose-splitting smell. "*Aaargh!* It's a skunk!"

Rabbit and Tuck giggled as Little John raced around the cell, clutching his beak. Finally he grabbed the bars and ripped the door off its hinges in a desperate attempt to escape the evil pong!

"This way!" shouted Rabbit.

Up the steps they all chased, along the castle wall and then a long dive into the moat. They swam to the far bank and clambered out, gasping.

From the castle, the Sheriff and Daffy hurled carrots at them in temper. But passing villagers picked them up and threw them back, shouting, "*Keep* your carrots. We're sick of 'em!"

And guess what Rabbit and his Merry Men feasted on when they returned to their forest camp! Carrots? *No fear!* Pepe Le Pew cooked a delicious omelette — French style!

Yawn...a fine morning! Hmm, I remember putting this knot in my blanket to remind me of something important today...

Morning, Bugs!

Mornin' Porky! You'll be putting on **MORE** weight eating like that. Hmm, was I going to start dieting?

Ch-Cheek!

BEEP, BEEP!

YIKES!!

'BEEP, BEEP' eh? Mmm, maybe I meant to have the horn fixed on my car!

Top of the...ah say, top of the morning to you, Bugs!

Could **THAT** be it? A resolution to stop repeating myself?

??

Tweet, tweet, t-weet!

Singing lessons? Did I mean to learn to sing properly— instead of like **TWEETY**?

Getting ready for your next voyage, Sam?

Maybe it's a hair-cut I need...

You got it, Bugs!

The Show Must Go Off!

It was the afternoon of the Grand Talent Competition in the village hall, and the compère was the famous local celebrity, Mr Bugs Bunny!

"Welcome, everyone!" announced Bugs genially. "We've plenty of exciting acts trying to win this super hamper of food . . . so let's get on with the show. First of all, it's Professor Sylvester, the world-famous birdsong impressionist!"

The audience clapped as Sylvester strode on stage, looking magnificent in his top hat and tail coat. They cheered as he proceeded to tweet just like a real bird. But then he dropped his microphone, and as he bent down to pick it up, his top hat fell off, revealing that it was Tweety, sitting on his head, doing the singing!

"Thank goodness I've escaped!" twittered Tweety. "Dat naughty puddy-tat kept me prisoner under his hat!"

"Boo! Hiss!" cried the audience.

"Thank you, Sylvester . . . and . . . er . . . Tweety too!" said Bugs, running onstage as the miserable cat sloped off. "And now, look above your heads and watch Balancing Foghorn Leghorn!"

Overhead a thin tightrope

stretched across the hall. At one end stood Foghorn in a glittering waistcoat studded with sequins. He bowed deeply and said, "Silence, please! Ah say, silence, please!"

Then, with wings flapping gently, he stepped gingerly along the rope. The audience was delighted – until the rope snapped! But instead of tumbling on to the people below, Foghorn kept on walking in mid-air!

"He's not *balancing* – he's just flying!" yelled a man.

"Twister!" shouted an old lady. "Get 'im off!"

So poor old Foghorn flapped off in disgrace without so much as another "Ah say"!

"Never mind, folks, the show gets better from now on,"

announced Bugs, "thanks to The Incredible Porko, who will now attempt to eat fifty pies in one minute!"

The curtain rose to reveal Porky Pig sitting at a small table piled high with pies. He smiled, held a large stopwatch high in the air and pressed the button to start it. But even before he had time to gobble his first pie, the audience grew angry once more.

"Huh!" shouted a boy on the first row. "That's nothin'. Porky eats pies that fast all the time!"

Porky, in a rage, picked up an armful of pies and pelted the audience with them! Then he made his getaway before they had time to throw them back!

"*Stop* – please stop!" cried

"I say, I say, I say," said Sam.

"Oh, dear," interrupted Pepe. "You sound just like Monsieur Foghorn Leghorn! Ho, ho! Hee, hee!"

Sadly the audience didn't find this joke funny, and Pepe began to panic. "Sam, mon ami, did you 'ear zee one about zee . . . um . . . zee . . . er . . ." Pepe's mind had gone blank, and the scared skunk began to make his dreadful scent.

"Aaargh!" cried the audience, gasping for air. "Phew! Send him back to France, for Pete's sake!"

Bugs, dodging the pies. "It's time to see death-defying Daffy Divalot dive from this fifty metre tower into a paddling pool . . ."

"A duck in a paddling pool?! How *unusual*!" jeered a man.

Daffy Duck, in a silly, tight bathing cap, climbed the ladder and then took fright! "Oh, no, I knew I'd forgotten something. I'm scared of heights!"

"Finally," said Bugs nervously, "two very fine comedians: Yosemite and Le Pew!"

Yosemite Sam and Pepe Le Pew marched on and began their act.

APPLAUSE-METER

100
90 10
80 20
70 30
60 40
50

Bugs put on a brave smile and wheeled the big applause-meter on to the stage.

"Ladies and gentlemen, it's time to show your appreciation for today's fabulous entertainers and decide who gets the super prize! Let's hear your applause for Professor Sylvester!"

Nothing! Not a single clap for the cunning cat!

"Now — Balancing Foghorn Leghorn!"

Nothing, except a cheeky cry of, "Rubbish!"

"How about The Incredible Porko?"

Nothing, except a pie thrown at the applause-meter!

"Daffy Divalot?"

Again, nothing.

"Yosemite and Le Pew?"

Silence, except a shout for some air-freshener!

Bugs didn't know what to do. He tried to look cheerful and said, "Well, that's all, folks. It's goodbye from your ol' pal Bugs Bunn . . ."

As soon as he said *his* name, the hall thundered with loud clapping, and the applause-meter went haywire!

"*You've* won," shouted the audience. "You deserve the prize for putting up with those useless acts!"

And so Bugs presented himself with the prize! Was that mean of him? Not really, because when the audience had left, he closed the doors and cheered up his sad friends by sharing his hamper feast with them!

Bugs makes a HORROR MOVIE!

Gweat place you've found for my howwor movie! I'm almost too scared to go ashore!

Boy, Bugs, this will be a b-blockbuster of a film with stars l-like you and Honey Bunny!

Yes, I daresay it will!

It's such a DELIGHT to work with Bugs!

Ready when you are, boss! Ah say, ready when you...

SHHHH!...ACTION!

What a strange place this lonely island is! Some say it's haunted by fiends and vampires...but I don't believe it!

WOO-OOOO!

AARGH! A vampire bunny!

Help me!

WOO-OOO!

What BWILLIANT acting!

Space Rabbit to the Rescue!

Space Commander Bugs Bunny had been called to an emergency meeting with some very important people, including the Prime Minister and the President of the United States!

"You brought me here to watch satellite TV?" complained Bugs, chewing idly on a carrot.

"That's right," said the President, flicking a switch on the video. "But wait till you see it!"

The screen came to life. A cartoon show began but then it was interrupted by loud crackles and the dim picture of a strange little shiny-suited man with a big head!

The sound was poor, but the creature could be heard saying, "*Planet Earth . . . great danger . . . invasion from space . . .*"

"You've got to investigate!" cried the Prime Minister. "Only *you* can help!"

"Okay, Doc," grinned Bugs. "Television repairman I ain't, but saving the world, well, that's a piece of cake!"

Commander Bugs and co-pilot Porky Pig cruised smoothly through the carrotsphere, far above Earth.

"Only another 36,000 miles to the TV satellite," sighed Bugs. "Anything to report?"

"N-nothin' special," replied Porky, peering through his laser-binoculars. "Only C-Coyote chasing Road Runner across the craters of the moon."

"Gee, those guys get *everywhere*!" replied Bugs.

"And there's a peculiar crate f-floating around loose. It has a label saying: Do not open — ever!"

"Hmm," mumbled Bugs mysteriously. "I'll bet I know what's in that . . ."

Presently they hovered over the satellite. Everything looked in order, except for a long wire trailing from it and leading to an old space-station, which looked more like a crumbling log-cabin drifting in space!

"Better take a look at that shack," suggested Bugs.

"Who? M-me?" stammered Porky. "But I'm scared of the dark!"

"It's hardly dark! The Sun's only 93 million miles away!" exclaimed Bugs. "Okay, I'll be right with you."

They put on their goldfish-bowl helmets and jetted from their star-cruiser to the space-station.

Zap! A laser beam zipped over the heads of Bugs and Porky. They ducked down and took a peep.

From the doorway came the sinister figure they had seen on TV back on Earth. It was Elmer Fudd!

"Stop, Elmer! It's me!" yelled

Bugs. "Now, what's all this about invading Earth?"

"Oh, sowwy, Bugs. I thought you were one of *them*!" Elmer pointed to a huge purple fog nearby. "I hooked up to the satellite to warn Earth of the danger fwom the aliens over there!"

"Oh, how p-pretty!" declared Porky, admiring the fog.

"You think so?" asked Elmer. "Well, dwive into it and you'll have a weal shock!"

Bugs and Porky did as Elmer told them, and they *did* have a shock! The purple fog was a clever decoy, for inside it was a huge laser-cannon under construction! Hundreds of ghastly little aliens with mean faces were swarming all over it, tightening nuts and bolts and connecting up cables.

Worst of all, the dreaded weapon was pointing directly at Planet Earth!

"Oh, dear, looks like t-trouble!" groaned Porky.

"Worried?" replied Bugs with a smirk. "Follow me and we'll soon have the problem solved."

With Porky at his side, Bugs jetted back out of the cloud and zoomed off into space, past Elmer and past the space-station.

"Now, where *was* that crate we saw drifting around . . ." murmured Bugs. "Ah, there it is! Straight ahead."

Although Porky had no idea what Bugs' plan was, he helped him to weave a long rope round the mysterious crate and tow it back to the purple fog.

"Get ready to scoot, Porks!" shouted Bugs, flicking open the catch on the door of the crate.

Before he raced off with Bugs, Porky caught sight of the door as it burst open and there, in a fearsome temper, stood *the Tasmanian Devil*!

Bugs and Porky returned to Elmer's space-station and waited for the fun to begin. Seconds later there were terrifying extra-terrestrial screams and a horrible crunching of metal being eaten! Aliens and bits of broken machinery came whizzing out of the cloud as the Tasmanian Devil chomped away at the laser-cannon!

"I guessed he'd enjoy a hearty meal!" grinned Bugs. "But we'd better disappear fast. You, too, Elmer. I think he may fancy your space-station as a dessert!"

"Gweat! I was fed up in space anyway," said Elmer, collecting his belongings together. "There are no wabbits up here to hunt!"

On their journey back to Earth, the radio crackled and the voice of the Prime Minister came through: "Space Commander, have you had any success?"

"Course I have!" laughed Bugs. "Mission accomplished. Earth's safe again. All in a day's work for ol' Bugs!"

"How can we ever repay you?" asked the Prime Minister.

"That's easy, Doc. Lay on some fresh carrots. I'm *starving*!"

Well, that's all for now, folks! Oh, not quite all . . .
I nearly forgot about the photograph we took!
Not bad, eh? The fact that me an' my pals put our
heads through the wrong holes has made
it better than ever!

Hope you enjoyed the book. See you again soon!

Answers to puzzles